Each of you should look not only

to your own interests but

also to the interests of others.

—Philippians 2:4

ZONDERKIDZ

The Berenstain Bears Hurry to Help
Previously published by Reader's Digest Kids in 1993 as *The Berenstain Bears and the Good Deed*
Copyright © 1992, 2010 by Berenstains, Inc.
Illustrations © 1992, 2010 by Berenstains, Inc.

Requests for information should be addressed to:

Zonderkidz, *Grand Rapids, Michigan* 49530

Library of Congress Cataloging-in-Publication Data

Berenstain, Stan, 1923-2005
   The Berenstain Bears hurry to help / created by Stan and Jan Berenstain ; with
Mike Berenstain.
      p. cm.
   Summary: While trying to earn their Good Deed Merit Badges, Bear Scouts Brother, Sister, and
Cousin Fred do more harm than good, but persevere and finally find someone who needs their help.
   ISBN 978-0-310-71938-0 (hardcover)
   [1. Scouting (Youth activity)—Fiction. 2. Christian life—Fiction. 3. Bears—Fiction.]
I. Berenstain, Jan, 1923- II. Berenstain, Michael. III. Title.
   PZ7.3.B4483Bemkn 2010
   [E]—dc22
                                              2009037062

All Scripture quotations, unless otherwise noted, are taken from the Holy Bible, *New International Version®, NIV®.* Copyright © 1973, 1978, 1984 by Biblica, Inc™. Used by permission of Zondervan. All rights reserved worldwide.

Any Internet addresses (websites, blogs, etc.) and telephone numbers printed in this book are offered as a resource. They are not intended in any way to be or imply an endorsement by Zondervan, nor does Zondervan vouch for the content of these sites and numbers for the life of this book.

Zonderkidz is a trademark of Zondervan.

Editor: Mary Hassinger
Art direction: Cindy Davis

Printed in China

10 11 12 13 14 15 /LPC/ 28 27 26 25 24 23 22 21 20 19 18 17 16 15 14 13 12 11 10 9 8 7 6 5 4 3

The Berenstain Bears

Hurry to Help

by Stan and Jan Berenstain
with Mike Berenstain

ZONDERVAN.com/
AUTHORTRACKER
follow your favorite authors

ZONDERKIDZ

Living
Lights™

It was going to be a big day for Bear Scouts Brother, Sister, and Cousin Fred. Today was the day they were going to get their Good Deed Merit Badges.

"Ready, Scouts?" said Scoutmaster Papa. "Let's go out and do a good deed."

"But first," said Brother, "we must find somebody to do a good deed *for*."

"That will be easy," said Papa. "There will be lots of bears who will need help today. I can feel it in my bones. Follow me, Scouts!"

Mama Bear gave them a little blessing, and a reminder to be like the Good Samaritan.

And off they went to find somebody to do a good deed for.

"Look!" said Papa. "Old Miz McGrizz is having trouble crossing the street! A perfect chance to do a good deed and get your merit badges."

"We're coming, Miz McGrizz!"
shouted Papa. "We will help
you cross the street!"

"Stop!" shouted Miz McGrizz. "I don't *want* to cross the street. I was waiting for a bus. Look! Now I've missed it!"

"Sorry about that," said
Papa as Miz McGrizz chased
them down the street.

"Do not worry, Scouts," said Papa. "We will find somebody to do a good deed for."

"Look!" he shouted. "Farmer Ben has fallen from his tractor, and the tractor is running away! A perfect chance to do a good deed and get your merit badges. Hurry! You go help Farmer Ben, and I'll stop the tractor."

But Farmer Ben didn't *need* help.
"I didn't fall," he said. "I'm just resting,
Scouts. You know what the Good Book
says...there is a time for everything."

Papa got a big log and threw
it in front of the runaway tractor.

But the tractor wasn't running away.
It was being driven by Mrs. Ben.
"What do you think you're doing,
Papa Bear?" said Mrs. Ben.
"Just trying to do a good deed,"
said Papa.

"Humph!" said Mrs. Ben.

"Good deed, indeed!" said Farmer Ben.

"Maybe we'd better go home and try again tomorrow," said Scout Sister.

"A real Bear Scout never quits!" said Scoutmaster Papa. "I know we're going to find someone to do a good deed for soon. Jesus says, 'He who searches will find.' I can feel it in my bones."

"Look! Up ahead!" Papa shouted. "Our friend Actual Factual is being attacked by bees! A perfect chance for you to get your merit badges.

"We're coming!" shouted Papa. He took
a bug bomb from his pack. He sprayed the
bees that were attacking Actual Factual.

But the bees were *not* attacking Actual Factual. They were *his* bees. He was their beekeeper. Actual Factual did not get angry. Actual Factual never got angry. But the bees did. The bees got very angry.

They chased Papa. It's a good thing he found a pond to jump into or those angry bees would have stung him.

"Oh, dear," said Sister. "We will never get our merit badges."

"Every time we try to do a good deed we get into trouble," said Scout Fred.

"But not this time!" shouted Papa. "Look up on the edge of that cliff. That car is in trouble. I can feel it in my bones! Follow me!"

But when they got to the top of the mountain, the car was not in trouble.

"We're just enjoying the lovely view of God's creation," said the bears in the car.

The scouts looked at Papa. Papa looked at the scouts. "Well, you see," said Papa...

That's when Papa slipped and fell.

Down,
down,
down the
mountain he rolled,
onto the
town dump at the foot
of the mountain.

"I don't feel so good," said Papa. "My leg hurts. My arm hurts. I hurt all over. I can feel it in my bones."

"Papa is hurt," said Sister. "How will we ever get him home?"

"Look!" said Brother. He was pointing at an old wheelbarrow that somebody had thrown away. The scouts helped Papa into the wheelbarrow.

It wasn't easy. Papa was heavy. But those three scouts pushed and pulled until at last they got Papa home.

The scouts were sad.

"Why are you sad?" asked Mama Bear.

"Because we didn't get our Good Deed Merit Badges," said Sister.

"We couldn't find anyone to do a good deed *for,*" said Brother.

"Well, it seems to me," said Mama, "that you *have* done a good deed. You got Papa home. Just like one of those special letters that Timothy wrote, '...good works are easy to see. But even good works that are hard to see can't stay hidden.'"

"Your mama's right," said Papa. "I can feel it in my bones."

And he gave the Bear Scouts their Good Deed Merit Badges right then and there.